DAN'S PANTS
The Adventures of Dan, the Fabric Man

Merle Good *with* Dan and Fran Boltz
Illustrated by Cheryl Benner

Intercourse, PA 17534
800/762-7171
www.goodbks.com
Printed in Hong Kong
C.I.P data may be found on page 32.

A tall and funny guy was he,
our Dan, the Fabric Man,
with legs so long and strong that he
was twice as high as Fran.

For Fran, the pretty wife of Dan,
was short and hard to kiss,
When he bent down, she clowned around,
and laughed when he would miss!

He'd call on every fabric store
to show his newest lines,
With bugs and slugs and birds and beasts
and flowers of all designs.

But Dan tonight was sorta sad,
for this was not his day,
A dog named Peg had nipped his leg
and ripped his pants away.

BUTTONS

To cheer him up, his Fran stayed up
    and stitched and sewed all night
To make some pants for Dan to wear—
    Oh, they were quite the sight.

When Dan stepped out in his new pants
to go from store to store,
The traffic stopped to toot and hoot
and cheer for what he wore.

DELI
le Hairtique
SEW WHAT FABRIC
SWEET STU
TAXI
Side Walk Cafe
SPECIALS

And Dan would wave and shake his legs
in pants of circus ponies,
or flying pigs or something strange
that looked like macaronis.

As years went by, his Fran made more,
which Dan would proudly wear,
From Empire State to Amish store,
exceeding ninety pair.

And animals would gather round
to see Dan's fruits and fishes,
his yellow yaks or turquoise toads—
They called him "Pantalicious"!

Except the bees who thought the blooms
were real—and so they chased
the pants of Dan, their "honey man,"
who raced away in haste.

FABRIC
MEETING 5:00
RING BELL
PROJECT SHOW 'N TELL TODAY
THREAD BLOW OUT SALE

The bolts of Boltz were used for quilts,
for kitty cushion covers,
for tablecloths, for shirts and skirts,
and bibs for ice cream lovers.

Some women shoppers liked to touch
the pants of Dan the Man,
They'd squeeze the fabric carefully,
congratulating Fran.

JUST
MARRIED

A customer he'd known for years
was married in her town,
The bride surprised him with some pants
that matched her maiden's gown!

And even Peg, who bit his leg,
began to like his pants.
She wagged her tail and flicked her ears
and jigged a little dance!

The Story of the Fabrics

Shown on these two pages are photographs of several of the fabrics Dan Boltz chose for some of his pants. Dan explains why he likes each fabric.

Floral

Who said only women could wear floral prints? Printed using flatbed screens, the black ground and rich colors give an almost tapestry look to this Hoffman fabric.

Kittens

A cuddly print on cotton sheeting from Concord's Makower line. Fran loves cats and kittens so Dan chose this fabric as a concession to her. After all, she makes all his pants. When she sews, their two cats like to lie on the fabric. They may have thought they saw some distant cousins on this pair.

Butterflies and Moths

Guaranteed to lighten anyone's step. This home decorating print from Concord, vat dyed on sailcloth, looks great as upholstery on a sofa, but even better as pants.

Log Cabin

Since most of the fabric Dan sells goes into quilts, this very popular quilting pattern holds a special charm. With its shapes and colors this beautifully engineered print from Hoffman seems to "move" and is a natural for pants.

Cardinals

As a long-time bird-watcher and feeder, Dan was drawn to this print. The careful artwork and fine detail is further enhanced by the Bokashi printing technique that Hoffman often uses. This fabric makes perfect pants for Christmas functions.

Critters

This whimsical Hoffman print brings out the child in all of us. These "turquoise toads" are mentioned in this book. The background mottling is a technique often used by Hoffman and serves to enhance the depth of the print.

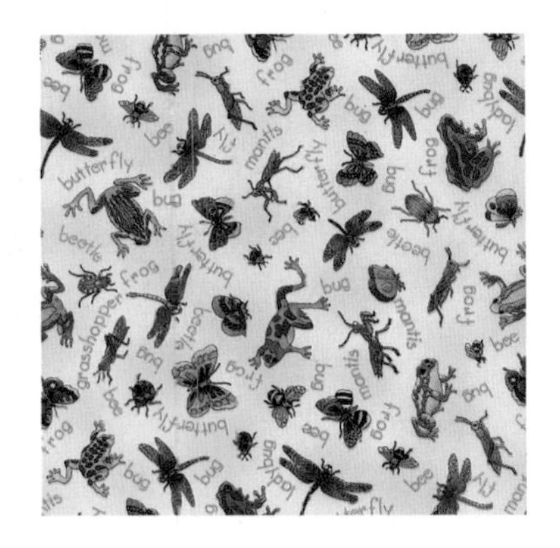

Bali

This unique Hoffman print, produced in Bali on cotton lawn, illustrates the many layers of hand batiking, painting, dyeing, and spritzing that are applied to this fabric to achieve this desired effect.

Grapes

One of Hoffman's all-time favorites. The print has been released many times. This perennial favorite on cotton sheeting still holds the gold outlines after nine years of washings.

Special thanks to Hoffman California Fabrics and to Concord Fabrics Inc. for their permission and help with this book.

About the Authors

Merle Good has authored numerous books, including the Reuben children's book series—***Reuben and the Quilt, Reuben and the Fire,*** and ***Reuben and the Blizzard***. He and his wife Phyllis are the storekeepers of the historic Old Country Store in Intercourse, Pennsylvania. Their store offers a large fabric selection and that's how they met Dan and Fran Boltz.

Dan Boltz has sold fabric from store to store throughout Pennsylvania, New York, and New Jersey for many years, where he has been known as "the tall guy with the funny pants." Fran, a retired elementary school teacher, now also sells fabric—and still makes pants for Dan. The Boltzes live in Sussex, New Jersey.

About the Artist

Cheryl Benner is an artist and designer from New Holland, Pennsylvania. She has illustrated several children's books, including ***The Boy and the Quilt***.

Design by Dawn J. Ranck
Cover illustration by Cheryl Benner

DAN'S PANTS: THE ADVENTURES OF DAN, THE FABRIC MAN

International Standard Book Number: 1-56148-307-9
Library of Congress Catalog Card Number: 00-034770

Printed in Hong Kong.

Library of Congress Cataloging-in-Publication Data

Good, Merle.
Dan's pants : the adventures of Dan, the fabric man / Merle Good with Dan and Fran Boltz ; illustrated by Cheryl Benner.
p. cm.
Summary: Everyone enjoys Dan's funny-looking pants, which his wife makes from the bright fabrics Dan sells. Includes photographs of different types of fabric.
ISBN 1-56148-307-9
[1. Pants--Fiction. 2. Textile fabrics--Fiction. 3. Stories in rhyme.]
I. Boltz, Dan. II. Boltz, Fran. III. Benner, Cheryl A., ill. IV. Title.
PZ8.3.G588Dan 2000
[E]--dc21
00-034770
CIP